to olivia
and to all the magical moments ahead!

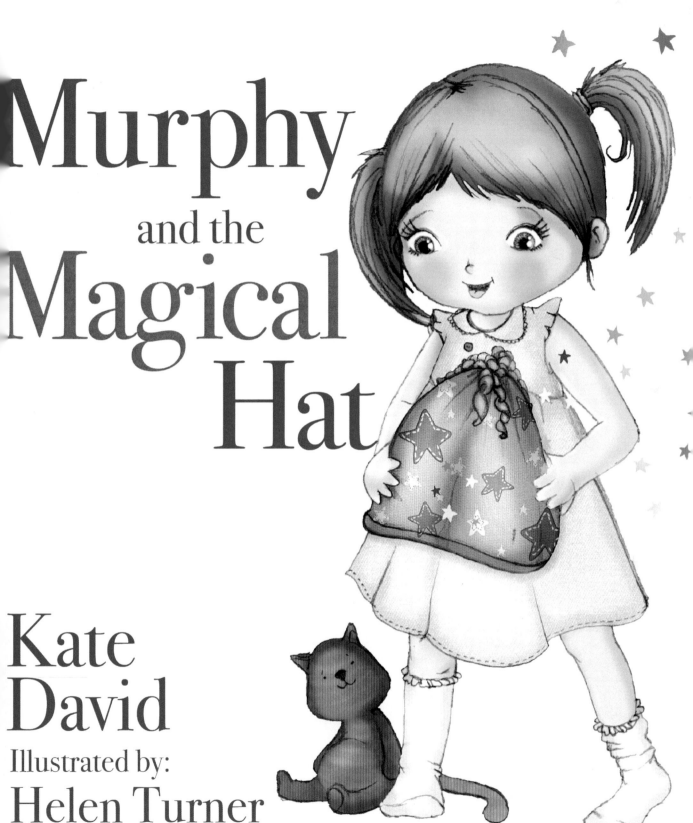

Murphy
and the
Magical
Hat

Kate
David
Illustrated by:
Helen Turner

Murphy and the Magical Hat
All Rights Reserved.
Copyright © 2012 Kate David
Illustrations © 2012 Helen Turner
v3.0

Outskirts Press, Inc.
http://www.outskirtspress.com

ISBN: 978-1-4327-8582-6

Outskirts Press and the "OP" logo are trademarks belonging to Outskirts Press, Inc.

PRINTED IN THE UNITED STATES OF AMERICA

To Murphy and Jeff who have
made my life magical. –Kate

For Eve, Mabel, Alice and Huey who bring
lots of magical moments to my life. –Helen

Murphy woke from her nap
eager to play outside.

She looked out through her bedroom window
and saw big raindrops falling from the sky.

Disappointed, Murphy stood in her
Mother's doorway with her shoulders
drooped and a hopeless look on her face.

"I'm sorry you can't play outside, but, I have a surprise for you that might cheer you up," her Mother said.

She reached into the
trunk at the foot of the
bed as Murphy watched
with anticipation.

"When I was a little
girl," her Mother said,
"your Nana gave me
this magical hat for
days just like today.
All I had to do was put
it on and I could go
anywhere I imagined!"

Murphy's eyes lit up.
She took the magical
hat and climbed up on
her Mother's bed.

Murphy thought about where she most wanted to go, and then placed the magical hat on her head.

She closed her eyes tightly and when she opened them...

She could feel grass between her toes, warm sunshine on her face and, in the distance, she could hear music.

As she ran through the park, the
music got louder and she could see
the horses going around and around.

The horses were part of a carousel
painted in beautiful colors.

*Red like a
cherry and
Blue like
the sea.*

*Yellow like
a lemon
and Green
like a tree.*

Brown like chocolate and Pink like bubble gum.

Orange like a pumpkin and Purple like a plum.

Murphy ran up to the entrance. She could hardly wait for the carousel to stop turning.

Finally, the gate opened and she quickly climbed up on a horse decorated in her favorite colors. The floor began to move under her and she started to spin.

Murphy giggled
with delight.
She was exactly
where she
had wanted to
be today.

After what seemed like hours of spinning, Murphy climbed down and began her journey back home through the park.

She lifted the hat
off her head and
opened her eyes.

Murphy felt the feathery pillow behind her
and instantly knew she was back home.
She was excited to tell her Mother
all about her magical afternoon.

"Where can I go tomorrow?" Murphy
asked her Mother. "Wherever your
imagination will take you!"

CPSIA information can be obtained
at www.ICGtesting.com
Printed in the USA
BVXC01n1838200814
363532BV00002B/2

* 9 7 8 1 4 3 2 7 8 5 8 2 6 *